BILLY THE BULLY
BRINGS IT BETTER

Written by
Roger F. Hartwich Jr., M.S.E., M.S.

Illustrated by
Nadia Ronquillo

First Print Edition

Copyright @ 2022 RFH-RLP Real Life Publishing, LLC

Disclaimer: This publication contains materials primarily for educational and informational purposes. The author and publisher have made earnest effort to ensure that the information in this book was correct at publication time and do not assume and hereby disclaim any liability to any party for any loss, damage, or disruption caused by errors and omissions.

Cover and Interior Design by Nadia Ronquillo

ISBN: 978-1-7362828-4-7

Table of Contents

Preface

Introduction

Contents and Main Events

Afterword: Author Comments

Worksheet: Discussion Questions

About the Author

Preface

This book was written to explain about bullying, a serious problem which sometimes happens to children. The author, a teacher for many years, writes from personal experience as a young person, as well as having seen, taught, or known young people who have been bullied in school. Bullying, whether physical, verbal, social or relational, can affect a person's emotional and social well-being, should be prevented if possible, and cannot be tolerated.

Introduction

Have you ever been bullied, or known someone who has been bullied? How does a person feel when they get bullied? What effects does bullying have on another person that has been bullied? This realistic fiction book is about a bully named Billy, a 3rd grade student, what he does to bully others, how it affects others, when he stops bullying, and the lesson he learns about how to treat others.

Billy the bully was in the 3rd grade. He was not nice to his classmates.
He tried to control them and make them feel

ANGRY, HURTFUL,
AND FRIGHTENED.

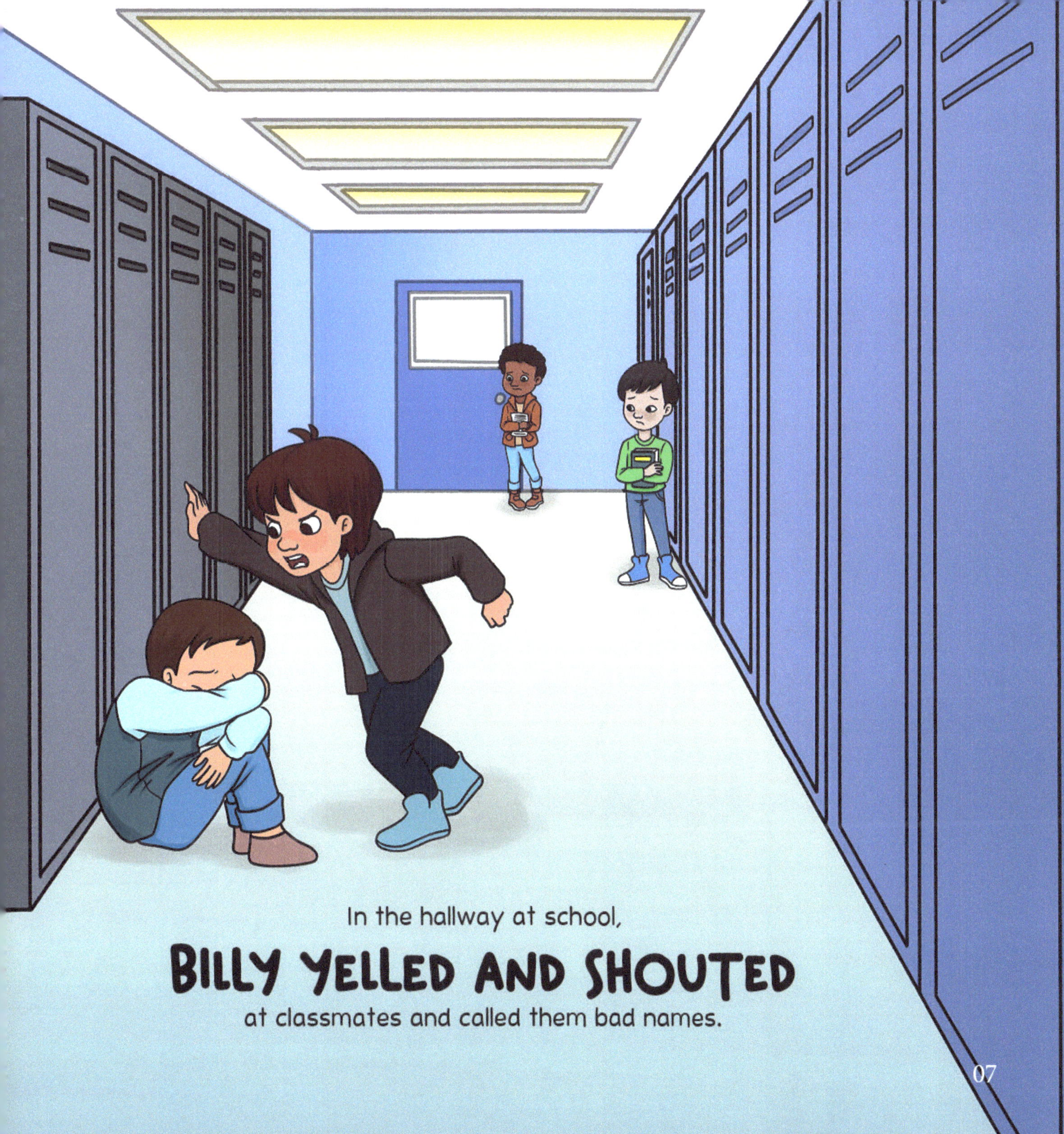
In the hallway at school,
BILLY YELLED AND SHOUTED
at classmates and called them bad names.

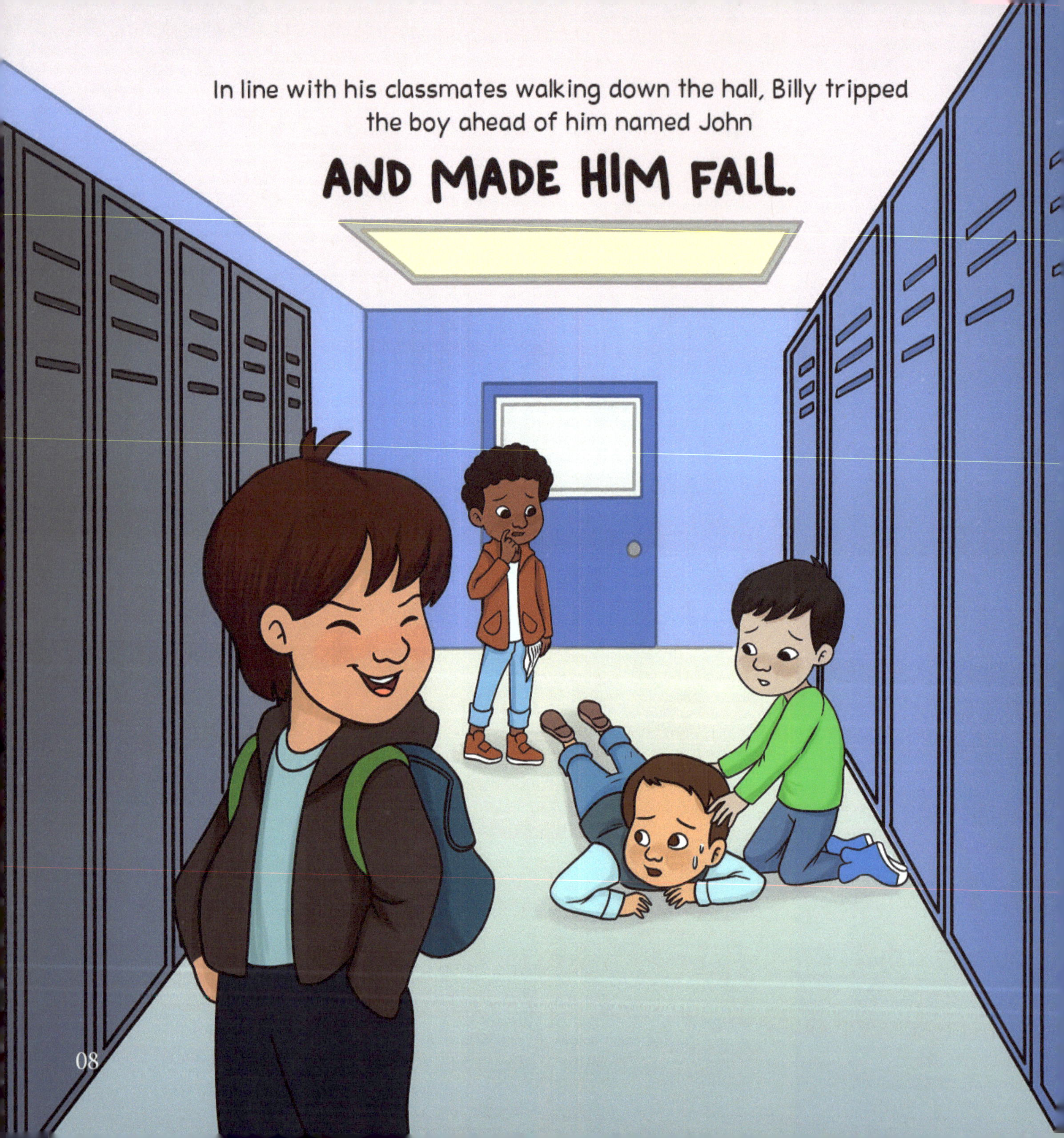

In line with his classmates walking down the hall, Billy tripped
the boy ahead of him named John

AND MADE HIM FALL.

In the lunch line in the cafeteria,
BILLY "BUDGED" AND PUSHED
classmate named Jim out of the line ahead of him.
Billy called out to Jim,
"YOU WEAK, SKINNY WIMP."

At lunch sitting at a table with other students in the cafeteria,
Billy put a carrot in Jenny's milk and a banana peel in her hair. He said to her,

In class sitting at his desk, Billy blurted and interrupted the teacher, Ms. Brown. Billy yelled and called her a bad name, and said
SHE WAS A VERY POOR TEACHER.

During reading class, Tommy was reading out loud and having difficulty pronouncing a word. Billy yelled at the boy,

"YOU CAN'T READ. YOU ARE DUMB! STUPID YOU!"

The boy felt very sad.

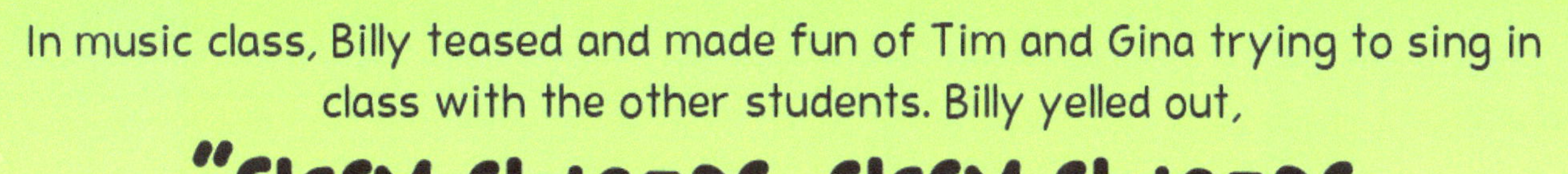

In music class, Billy teased and made fun of Tim and Gina trying to sing in class with the other students. Billy yelled out,

"SISSY SINGERS, SISSY SINGERS. YOU CAN'T SING!"

In art class, Billy made
BIG DARK MARKS AND SCRIBBLES
on his classmate Nolan's drawing. He also
SCRIBBLED BAD WORDS
on Nolan's drawing. Nolan felt angry and sad.

In gym class during kickball, Billy teased his classmate Bobby and called him lazy.

Billy threw the ball at Bobby, and it hit him in the head. He also yelled at a girl named Deb that was running the bases and said,

"YOU'RE TOO SLOW TO RUN THE BASES!"

On the playground, Billy liked to pick on a smaller boy named Mark.
HE KICKED, HIT, AND PUSHED MARK DOWN
while he was playing.
Billy cried out,
"YOU'RE A LITTLE WEAKLING."

On the bus,
BILLY YELLED AND SCREAMED AT THE BOY HE LIKED TO PICK ON NAMED MARK,
He said mean things about Mark, trying to make him feel bad. He also made rude remarks to the bus driver.

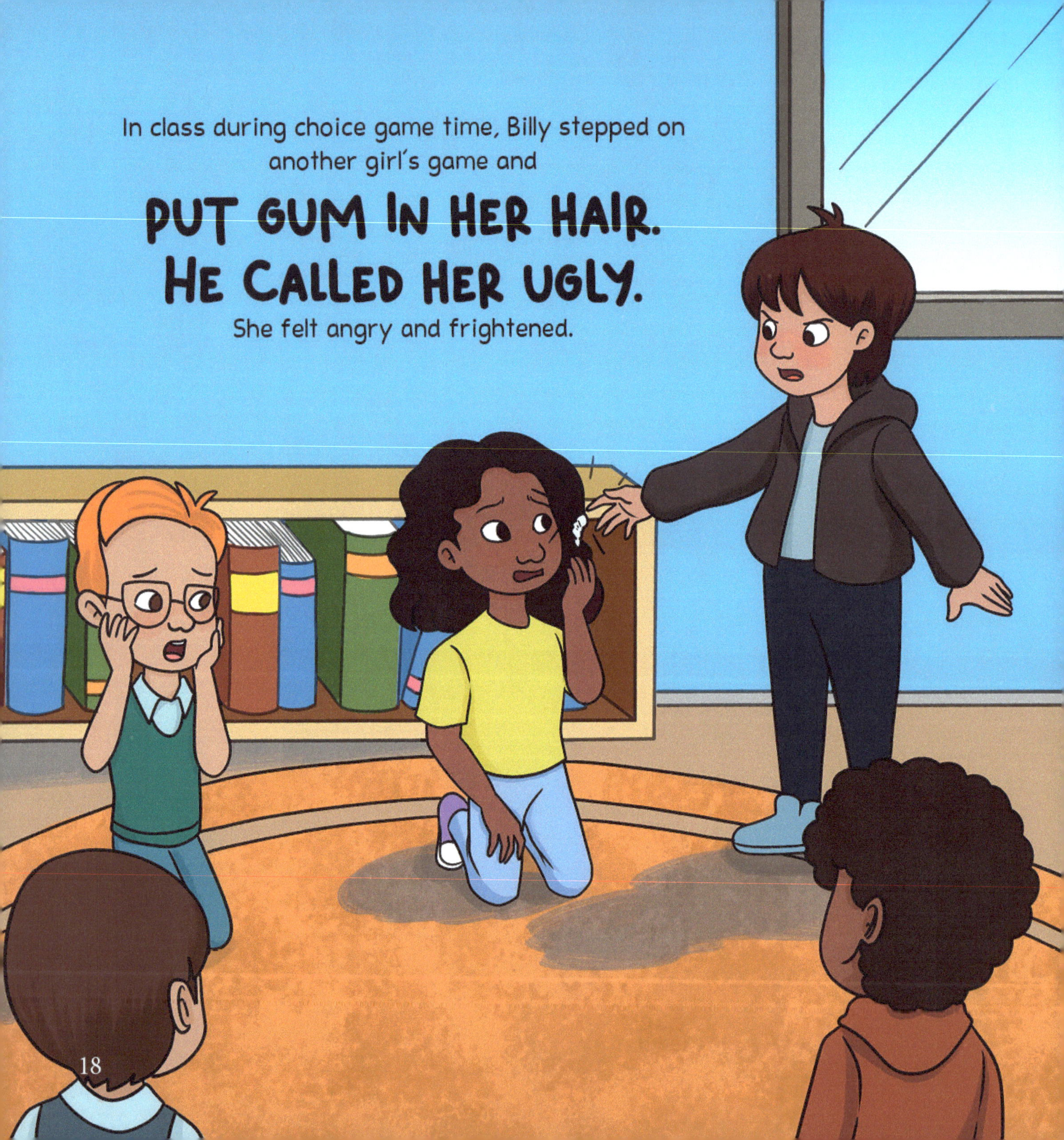

In class during choice game time, Billy stepped on
another girl's game and

PUT GUM IN HER HAIR.
HE CALLED HER UGLY.

She felt angry and frightened.

When his classmate named Brittany was trying to solve a math problem in class at her desk, Billy blurted and screamed,
"YOU'RE A LOSER AT MATH. YOU'RE STUPID."

In reading class, a visually impaired boy named Anthony was on the computer trying to read a story. Billy made fun of Anthony and called out to him,

"YOU CAN'T READ. YOU'RE DUMB!"
The boy felt very sad.

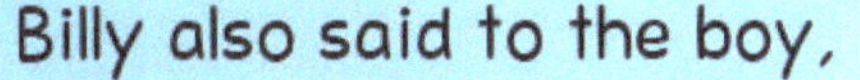

In writing class, a boy named Jeremy was trying to write a story.
Billy walked up to Jeremy's desk and made a racist remark about his looks.
Billy also said to the boy,

"YOUR WRITING IS NO GOOD!"

The boy felt very sad.

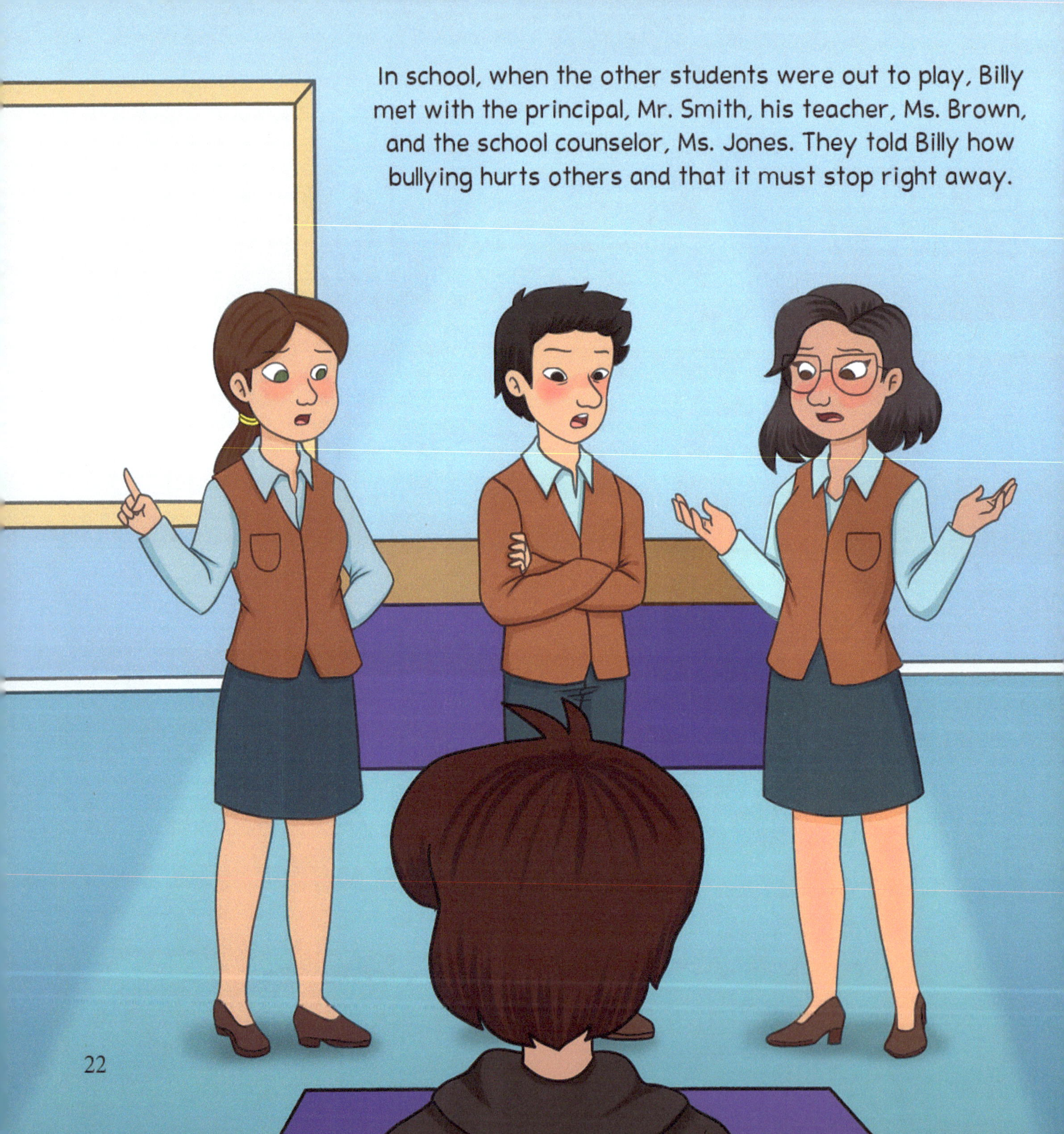

In school, when the other students were out to play, Billy met with the principal, Mr. Smith, his teacher, Ms. Brown, and the school counselor, Ms. Jones. They told Billy how bullying hurts others and that it must stop right away.

After school at the teacher's desk Ms. Brown called Billy's parents about his bullying and his inappropriate behavior. Ms. Brown and his parents agreed that Billy's bullying must stop right away.

When Billy was home for the weekend, he had a talk with his parents about bullying and that it must stop. Billy later went out for a bicycle ride on the street near his house. He had a serious bicycle accident, broke his leg, and had to go to the hospital. The doctor put his leg in a large cast.

Billy's parents called Billy's teacher about his bicycle accident. Billy's parents said they were very sorry for Billy's poor behavior. The teacher then told her class about Billy's serious bicycle accident.

Despite the way Billy had treated and bullied several of his classmates, his class decided to make and send get-well cards to Billy's home.

They hoped Billy's leg would heal quickly.

27

Billy received the get-well
cards at his home from
his classmates.
He felt very bad about being a bully at school and
the way he poorly treated his classmates
and his teacher.

Billy returned to school the next week with his leg in a cast. Billy spoke to his classmates,
"Thank you for the get-well cards. I am very sorry for being a bully."
He then passed out treats from home to all his classmates.
29

Billy then said to his classmates,

"I wish to become a good person and no longer be a bully.

From that day on, Billy was never a bully. He developed new friendships with classmates.

He was kind, respectful, and helpful to them,

to his teacher, the principal, and all other people. He became a very good person.

Afterward: Author's Closing Remarks

Bullying others, especially children, can be detrimental to their emotional, psychological, and social well-being, and personal development. Bullying is done on purpose and may happen repeatedly. It involves the abuse or imbalance of power to hurt others, when a child has a difficult time defending himself or herself. It may be done to try to humiliate another person.

Personally experienced first-hand, seen, or studied by the author, a teacher for many years, bullying is done in different ways. These include physical, verbal, social or relational, and stealing or damaging another person's property or belongings. Some bullies have previously been bullied themselves. The following are various types of bullying seen in school or other settings.

Physical bullying may involve kicking, hitting, pushing, or pinching to attack others, or unwanted sexual or physical contact. As seen by the author, boys may bully using more physical means.

Verbal bullying, the most common form of bullying, may involve use of derogatory words to harm others. These include insults, name calling, racial or other taunts, sexual comments, teasing, or mimicking another child. It may also include spreading untruthful gossip about others, harassing, and lying about another person or persons as an attempt to get them in trouble.

Social or relational bullying may involve excluding someone from a peer group. As seen by the author in school, an example might include a school child telling a classmate that he or she can't play with a group of children or telling other children not to play with a particular child, done with intent and sometimes done repeatedly to hurt someone. Social or relational bullying through social exclusion may most often be done by girls.

Ongoing, persistent bullying may result in negative effects on a bullied child including depression, low self-esteem, shyness, poor academic achievement, and isolation. They may become frightened, do poorly in their schoolwork, and become withdrawn. This especially pertains to youth who often get bullied and do not tell others about their getting bullied.

Bullying should be prevented or stopped immediately whenever it occurs, for the emotional, psychological, and social health and well-being of young people. It should be up to all of us to help prevent bullying, to stop it when it occurs, to encourage the bullied individual to tell an adult when it occurs, and to assist the individual in getting the help that they may need.

Discussion Questions

1. What are reasons for a person being a bully?

2. What is the first thing a person should do if he or she gets bullied?

3. What should a person do if he or she gets bullied? Who do you think a person should discuss this with if they get bullied?

4. What are some ways that bullies bully other people?

5. Discuss some negative effects bullying may have on a person that gets bullied. How might a bullied person feel and act?

6. How can bullying be prevented or stopped when it occurs?

7. What steps should you take if you get bullied?

8. How might a teacher, school counselor, social worker, and parents help a bully to stop being a bully, and to be respectful and kind to other people?

About the Author

Roger F. Hartwich Jr., M.S.E., M.S., B.S., B.A., has been a teacher and a landscaper/landscape designer/horticulturist/arborist for many years. Roger has taught full time K-12 Special Education in most disability areas, regular elementary education, and most subject areas including German as a substitute teacher. Roger is a small business owner in the field of horticulture/landscape technology and design and owns an independent (Indie) self-publishing LLC business. Roger has also worked in financial services for a short period of time.

Roger believes and writes in several different areas including environmental preservation, horticulture/trees and other plants, landscape design, and educational related topics.

Roger has written this book on bullying, an important topic and serious behavior which negatively affects others and may take place in various settings. Roger writes on subjects of special interest to educate, inspire, motivate, and entertain children, youth, and adults.

Roger is an Army veteran and former Navy Reservist, United States Navy Retired, with 20 years of military service. Roger holds Masters' Degrees in Special Education and Recreation and Park Administration, a B.S. Degree in Elementary Education, a B.A. Degree in Social Science, German minor, and a technical college degree in horticulture/landscape technology and design.

It is hoped that this book primarily for children and youth will help them, as well as adults, become aware of bullying, realize its possible negative effects on those being bullied, and realize the need to have bullying prevented and stopped.

Roger currently resides in Wisconsin.